The Crystal Unicorn

Story by Julie Mitchell
Illustrations by Beauville-York

PM Chapter Books
part of the Rigby PM Collection

U.S. edition © 2001 Rigby
a division of Reed Elsevier Inc.
500 Coventry Lane
Crystal Lake, IL 60014
www.rigby.com

Text © Nelson Thomson Learning 2000
Illustrations © Nelson Thomson Learning 2000
Originally published in Australia by Nelson Thomson Learning

06 05 04 03 02 01
10 9 8 7 6 5 4 3 2 1

The Crystal Unicorn
ISBN 0 7635 7451 1

Printed in China by Midas Printing (Asia) Ltd.

Contents

Chapter 1

A Terrible Thing

The moment I saw the little glass unicorn, I wanted it. It stood on a shelf in a corner of the jewelry store, and I had never seen anything so beautiful in my life.

I picked it up, and colored light flashed from its horn and legs.

"What kind of glass is this?" I asked Mom.

She turned from the jeweler. "It's crystal, Gina, and it's very expensive. You'd better put it back."

I looked at the price tag. Sixty-five dollars. It might as well have been a million.

I put the unicorn down, and felt a
dreadful longing. If only I could have it,
I'd never want anything else.

"Time to go, Gina," Mom said, then
she turned back to the jeweler.

I gazed at the unicorn for a few moments longer. Then I did a terrible thing: I took it from the shelf and put it in the pocket of my jacket. I was pretty sure no one saw me do it, but I felt a lot better once Mom and I left the store.

Chapter 2

The Trouble Begins

We went home on the train, and that's when the trouble started—everyone on our seat was so squashed together that the unicorn began to poke into my side.

If it was paid for, I thought, it would be wrapped in tissue paper. And it would be in a bag so it couldn't hurt me.

But I *hadn't* paid for the unicorn. And I would have to wait until I got home before I could even look at it again.

It was a long time before I had a chance. As soon as we got inside, Mom reminded me that it was Thursday night, and Mrs. Dobbs would soon be picking me up for gymnastics.

I quickly changed into my gym clothes, and in the rush, I left my jacket lying on my bed.

In the middle of gymnastics, I started worrying—perhaps Mom had hung my jacket up, and found the unicorn in the pocket! I couldn't think about anything else, and messed up every one of my tumbles.

When I got home, though, my jacket was still on the bed. Thank goodness!

I took out the unicorn, and right then, I heard footsteps outside my door!

Chapter 3

The Truth

"Time for dinner!" Mom called.

My heart banged in my chest. What if Mom had walked in and seen me with the unicorn! She'd know right away that I'd stolen it!

Quickly, I shoved it in a drawer, then I headed for the dining room.

All through dinner I thought about the unicorn. So far I hadn't been able to enjoy it; I was too busy trying to keep it hidden.

I wanted to put the unicorn on my dresser, but Mom would see it. I wanted to show it to my friends, but I couldn't do that, either. I couldn't even tell them about it.

Finally, I had to face the truth—I would never really be able to enjoy the little unicorn because it was stolen.

I put my fork down. Suddenly I wasn't hungry any more.

Mom looked hard at me.

"What's the matter, Gina?" she asked.

I felt my eyes fill with tears. "Oh, Mom, I've done a terrible thing. When we were in the jewelry store today, I took something."

"I know," she said sternly. "The little unicorn. I found it while you were out."

She looked right at me.

"I'm glad you told me about it, Gina. But you know there's only one way to put things right, don't you?"

"Yes," I said softly. "I'll have to take it back."

Chapter 4

The Apology

On Friday afternoon, I wrapped up the crystal unicorn and put it in a box. Then Mom and I went back to the jewelry store.

"Oh … hello," said the jeweler, as I stepped up to the counter.

I gave him the box containing the unicorn. "This is yours," I said quietly. "I took it when I was in here yesterday. I'm very sorry."

The jeweler opened the box and looked inside.

"Ah," he said. "The crystal unicorn. I noticed it was missing. I remembered how you'd admired it yesterday." He paused for a moment, watching me.

Mom went to wait by the door while I just stood there, wondering what the jeweler would do.

"I could call the police," he said. "But I'm pleased you brought it back yourself. Perhaps you don't know how much shoplifting costs everyone."

"No," I said, and shook my head. My face felt hot.

"I have to pay extra for insurance so that I can replace things that are stolen," continued the jeweler, "and for the security guards who patrol the mall."

"Oh," I said softly. "I didn't know that."

"And when I have to pay extra, I pass some of that cost on to my customers." He held up the crystal unicorn. "This is sixty-five dollars. But if people didn't steal, I could afford to charge less for it."

"Oh," I said again. I felt so ashamed.

"No, I won't call the police," said the jeweler, "because I know you realize you did the wrong thing."

Mom joined us. "Thank you for explaining things to Gina," she said to the jeweler. Then she turned to me. "Did you understand everything?"

I nodded.

We left the store, and went home in silence.

Chapter 5

Mom's Good Idea

Later that day, I found Mom working in the garden.

"I feel so embarrassed," I told her.

"It could have been a lot worse, Gina," she said. "If you'd been caught shoplifting, and the security guards weren't able to contact me, you would have been taken to the police station. And children who keep shoplifting end up in court."

When I heard that, I started to cry. "I'm really sorry, Mom. I won't *ever* do it again. I promise."

Mom hugged me.

"I just don't want any of those things to happen to you, Gina," she said. "And besides, there's no need for you to steal. If you see something you really want, you can always save up for it."

"But by the time I saved enough money for the unicorn, someone else would have bought it."

"I could put it on layaway for you," Mom said. "Then the jeweler puts it away until all the payments are made."

"How much would the payments be?" I asked.

"Oh, about ten dollars a week, I imagine."

I sighed. "Then that's no good. I only get five dollars a week for allowance."

"You could earn the extra five dollars a week," Mom suggested.

"How?"

"I'm sure if you ask around, you'll find lots of people who need odd jobs done. You could start with Mrs. Hooper, next door. Only yesterday she told me how badly her garden needs weeding."

I smiled. "And there's Mrs. Tan. She's always saying she doesn't have time to walk her dog as often as she needs to. Maybe I could walk the dog for her."

I was beginning to feel a lot better.

"I'll go and ask her now," I said. I kissed Mom, said "Thanks," and ran out the front gate.

Chapter 6

The Last Payment!

That was just the beginning. Over the next few weeks, I found lots of people who needed my help. I got busy weeding gardens, walking dogs, and washing cars. I even cleaned out a birdcage—and I didn't mind a bit!

In the meantime, Mom put the crystal unicorn on layaway. Each week we went to the jeweler's to make a payment on it.

Seven weeks later, Mom and I went to make the last payment.

"You've been working hard, Gina," the jeweler said, as I paid him the last five dollars.

"Yes," I said. "Thank you for keeping the unicorn safe for me."

I watched him wrap it in tissue paper, and put it in a pretty paper bag. And when he passed it to me, I grinned.

"Thank you," I said. "I have the perfect spot for it at home."

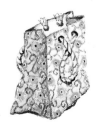

Later, I put the crystal unicorn on my dresser—right in the middle, for everyone to see.

It's still standing there. And when my friends come over, they enjoy making it sparkle in the light.

But not half as much as I do.